The Singing Fish

Peter Markus

Calamari Press

THE SINGING FISH

© Peter Markus 2005

All Rights Reserved.

ISBN 0-9746053-8-7

Cover Design: Derek White

Title Font: Eduardo Recife

A number of these fictions first appeared in the following publications:

"What the River Told Us To Do" in *Quarterly West* and was later reprinted in the anthology *Fiction Gallery* (Bloomsbury USA)

"When It Rains It Rains A River" in *La Petite Zine*

"What Our Mother Always Told Us" in *Avatar Review*

"We Eat Mud" in *SleepingFish*

"Boy" in *5_Trope*

"Fish Heads" in *LitRag*

"Boy: Revisited" in *elimae*

"Where There's Mud Only When It Rains" in *Opium*

"The Singing Fish," "The Singing Fish: Revisited," "Fish Heads: Revisited" and "Guts" in *taint*

Published by Calamari Press, New York, NY

www.calamaripress.com

CONTENTS

What The River Told Us To Do

We watched our father hammer and pound, into our front yard's ground, a handmade sign that said, in letters big enough for us brothers to read what it said, all the way down from where we were watching, down by the muddy river's muddy shore: HOUSE FOR SALE. We'd seen signs like this sign before, sticking up from the front yards of other people's houses, but never in the front of ours. We knew what happened to those people who hammered those signs, down into the ground in the fronts of their houses' front yards. After a while, those people with signs out in the fronts of their houses left away from our town and were soon replaced by new people who came to live on the insides of these kinds of houses. Us brothers, we did not want to be one of those people. We didn't want our house to be that kind of a house. Our house, we did not want it to be a house with anybody but us living inside it. But us brothers, we both knew that this— us living in some other house, in some other town, a town without a dirty river running through it, a town without so much mud and smoke and rust—this was what our mother said she wanted for the both of us. We'd heard her say, to our father, that it was either this house and this dirty river town, or it was her that was leaving. Us, our mother's dirty boys, we listened up close. We hoped we might one night hear the sound of footsteps leaving, a door opening, then closing, shut. Later on that day, when us brothers saw our father working on the making and the painting and the nailing together of that sign that said on it, HOUSE FOR SALE, we asked our father, what was he doing, then, what was it, the sign, for? We stood by and watched our father's mouth move around to make such sounds as *mother* and *river* and *town*. We watched our father raise up his hand and point with his first finger to where the mill was sitting dark and quiet on the river's muddy shore. But us brothers, we didn't want our ears to hear what it was that our father was wanting us sons to hear. And our eyes, when we looked upriver at the mill, it sitting silent and still, what we saw was the moon rising up big and white and glowing—the mill's rusted smokestacks holding it up. Us brothers said some words back to our father, words such as *moon* and *mud* and *river* and *fish*, but even these words, words that were the world to us brothers, these were sounds that our father did not hear. We watched our father drop his head back down so that he could see his right hand holding his hammer: in his other hand he held a handful of bent-back nails. When our father did this with his hands, us brothers did this with ours. We each of us took the other one of us by the hand and we went with each other down to the river, to ask the river: what should we, us brothers, do? When the river told us what to do, we both of us knew it was the only thing we could do. So that night, while our mother and our father were both of them in their room with the lights in their room turned off for sleeping, what we did was we climbed out through our bedroom's window. Only the moon and the stars were watching us that night as we walked out to our father's tool shed and got out his hammers and a box full of his rusty, bent-back nails. We each of us brothers took up a fist full of nails and a hammer into each one of our hands and we walked out back to the back of our backyard, back to where there was a telephone pole back there studded with the chopped off heads of fish. Brother, I said to Brother. You can go first. Brother, I told him, give me your hand. Hold your hand up against this pole. Brother did just what I told. We were brothers—we were each other's voice inside our own heads. This might sting, I warned. And then I raised back that hammer. I drove that rusty nail right through Brother's hand. Brother didn't even wince, or flinch with his body, or make with his boy mouth the sound of a brother crying out. Good, Brother, I said. I was hammering a second nail into Brother's other hand when our father stepped out into the yard. Us, our father's sons, we turned back with our heads toward the sound of our father. We stood like this waiting to hear what it was that our father was going to say to us brothers next. It was a long few seconds. The sky above the river where the steel mill stood shipwrecked in the mud, it was dark and silent. Somewhere, I was sure, the sun was shining. You boys remember to clean up before you come back in, our father said to us then. Our father turned back his back. Us brothers turned back to face back each other. I raised back the hammer. I lined up that rusted nail.

When It Rains It Rains A River

Other boys, when it rains, they run inside to be with their mothers, but us brothers, when it rains, we run outside to be with ourselves. Outside, in the rain, the dirt beneath us turns to mud. Us brothers, we love mud. Mud, us brothers, we can't get us enough of mud. We like to make mud, in the rain, out of the dirt, by doing what some boys might see as two brothers running in the rain. But us brothers, in the rain, this is not us just running around in the rain. In the rain, us boys, this is just the way us brothers fish. We fish, when it rains, and us brothers, in the rain, fishing like this, this makes the earth turn to mud. The rain, when it drums down on the tops of our boy heads, the sound of it falling, it makes music in our ears. We lift our hands, our mouths, up to the sky. Like this, with our hands held high, our faces facing the rain, us brothers, we start to sing. We sing and we sing and we do not stop singing until the rain stops drumming down. When the rain stops drumming down, us brothers, we drop down, onto our hands and knees, down in mud, and we begin to eat. We eat until our bellies are big with mud. We take what is left of the mud and we make Girl. We start at the bottom and make our way up. Girl's knees are especially muddy. They make us want to stay forever kneeling. If it looks as if we are on our knees saying our prayers, look again. We are watching Girl wake up. At night, when we look up from the mud with our mud-shot eyes, we see that the sky, it has floating up in it not one, but two, moons. These moons, they are what Girl uses to look at the world through. When Girl looks down to see the mud that she is made from, us brothers, we look up into Girl's eyes to see that each moon, it is a mirror. Inside each mirror, we see a girl, other than Girl, gazing back at us. These girls other than Girl, these other girls—these girls are Girl's sisters. There is a sister, we see, for each of us brothers. And so, us brothers, we raise ourselves up off of our hands and knees, out of the mud, and we dive inside. When we dive inside each of these moons, each moon shatters into a billion pieces. Each broken chunk becomes a star. Look here, Brother says. He points up with all ten of his stub fingers. The stars! Brother says. The stars are burning fish. Who says? I say to this. I shoot Brother this look. Us brothers, we have this look that we sometimes like to look at each other with. It's the kind of a look that actually hurts the face of the brother who is doing the looking. Imagine that look. Says me is who, Brother says to this. Oh yeah, I say. But who said so to you? What Brother says to this is he says: Girl. I don't say anything back to this. If Girl says that this is so, then, yes, this is so. The stars are burning fish. So then I take back that look. Look at us brothers now. Watch us brothers reach out to these burning fish fires with our hands mittened with mud. We stick our hands, unfisted, into this fire. We feel around, inside of fire, until we find fire's star-shaped heart. This fire, it is gill-plate sharp to our fingers' touch. It is five-armed, fifty-fingered. We pull back hard, we set the hook hard, on fire's sticking-out hands, until the whole sky is a river sparking with fire, until fire is all that we see. See us pull, see us pull, see us keep on with this pulling, until our hands explode in our face.

The Singing Fish

One night Girl is so sound asleep sleeping that her sleeping body, it becomes a cave, and us brothers, we climb inside. Inside, it is not dark inside. Inside, there is a light inside that does not shine from someplace outside. Outside, the moon, it is a fish swimming in some river that is unseen to us brothers and our mud-shiny eyes. Us brothers, what we see, inside this cave, we see pictures—stick-figure fish—on these mud-caved walls. These fish, stick-scrawled across made-out-of-mud walls—these fishes—they are pictures of us. These stick-figure fish with their round moon faces and with their stick-figure arms and stick-figure legs, their stick-figure fingers sticking out to the sides of their stick-figure chests—oh yes, these fish, they are us. And words, words! There are these words there, too—these words—they have got to be words. What else could these things be? Isn't every thing a word hidden and hiding as something else? These words that are scribbled and scrawled up and down and all across these made out of mud walls here on the inside of this cave—this cave that, this one night, Girl's sleeping body, this is what it becomes. Us brothers, we both know this. But these words—these things that look like words—these markings that are carved into these mud walls—they look too much *like* words not to *be* words. But these words, these words, what is it that these words mean, or say? What are these words trying to tell us? Us brothers, it's true that us brothers—this much we don't know, at least not yet. We cannot yet read them, these things that we call words. Not with our eyes and not with our ears do we hear what these words are saying. So what we do is this: we give it a try, to break in to what these things are saying—no, not with our eyes, our ears. No, we look at these words with our hands. We take these words into our hands. See us brothers lay our hands across these mud walls. Our hands with half-moons shining up and out from beneath these gnawed down to the knuckles nails. These hands that are stars, are starfish—these hands with knuckles that are rivers that run deep. These are the hands that us brothers, we touch them, our hands, up and down upon these made out of mud walls with these things—words—written on them. We close our eyes to let our hands do this seeing. This is what they see. They see *mud* and *fish* and *river*. They see *moon* and *brother* and *girl*. Our hands, us brothers, we keep on looking with our hands, and we do not stop looking until the words themselves—*mud* and *fish*, *moon* and *river*, *brother* and *girl*—they become bones. No, they are fingers. No, no, they then become: tongues. No, look again: they become fish. No, they are singing fish—picture it: singing fish!—singing in the rivers of our hands.

What Our Mother Always Told Us

What our mother always told us was, Don't, don't go, don't get muddy, don't walk into this house with mud, with mud wet, with mud caked dry, on the bottoms of your muddy boots. But us brothers, with our filled up with mud ears, we did not hear it when our mother said that word: don't. All we heard was our mother telling us brothers to go, get good and muddy, our mother's voice telling us, her dirty little boys, to walk into the house with mud wet, mud caked dry, on the bottoms of our muddy boots. What did I just tell you? This was the question, these were the words, that our mother was, to us brothers, all of the time saying to us. Us brothers, we wouldn't say anything to what it was that our mother was saying. We would stand there, with mud shining up on the floor between us, with mud in broken pieces, breadcrumbs of mud, scattered across the floor behind us, and we would wait then for what we knew was always about to come at us brothers next. What was about to come at us brothers next was this: our mother would come running at us brothers with her mother hands pinching towards us brothers until it was our ears, one ear for each of us brothers, that she had pinched in her pinching hands. Our mother's pinchy fingers, they did not make us flinch, or wince with our bodies, or make us with our boy mouths make the sound of a brother crying out for help. Bad, our mother would try to whisper to us, but the whisper of this would make more of a hiss. How many times, our mother would then say this, do I have to tell you no, don't, stop? You boys make it out like you got mud for brains, our mother liked to us brothers say. To this, us brothers, to our mother saying this to us, we would always say to her, Thank you. Our mother, she would not say anything to us saying thank you. She'd just pinch and tug and pull at our muddy boy ears until our boy heads were almost touching, and she would not stop this tug-of-war tugging until our faces were face-to-face facing the shining up at us whiteness of the bathroom's sink. And what she would do next was this: our mother, she would turn on the hissing hot water faucet, turn it on full blast, and she would then take into her mother hand a bristle-headed brush, the same brush she used to scrub the mud from off the bottoms of our boots, and then she would scrub at us brothers, she'd scrub at our muddy hands, she'd scrub at the mud that was crusted behind our ears, and she would not stop with this scrub-brush scrubbing until the sink that we were gazing down into, with hot water hissing out from its spout, turned from its shining whiteness to the rivery color of mud. The more mud that our mother scrubbed, the harder she pulled and tugged and brushed at us brothers with that bristled brush, the more muddy, the muddier, the water and the sink with the muddied water filling up inside of it would get. And after it was over, after our mother would send us to our bedroom, no matter how hard or for how long our mother would spend cleaning up after this muddy mess, there would always be some spatter of speckled mud, some smudgy stain of muddied-up water, left behind in our wake. And on nights like these, after our mother was in her own room fast asleep sleeping, us brothers, we'd crawl around the house on our hands and knees and, like this, we'd clean up, we'd lick, the left-behind mud up. Oh, this house, on nights like these, in those places where the mud had once been so muddy, this house, it never looked so shiny. No, not even our mother could have dreamed that a house made out of mud could ever be so clean.

We Eat Mud

One night us brothers, we got home from fishing fish out of the dirty river that runs its way through this dirty river town only to find our father there in the kitchen, our father standing where our mother so often always stood, in front of the stove, with his back looking back at us brothers, his face facing away from us brothers, and what it was he was doing, standing there like this, facing the stove, was he was fixing us up some supper. Mud cakes was what he said he was almost done cooking up, when we asked him what it was he was cooking up. And mud pies, too, our father said, and when he opened up the oven's door, when he did, a muff of muddy smoke came coughing out. Out was all that our father said to us brothers when we asked him where was our mother. Us brothers, the both of us, inside our boy heads, what we were wondering was, Out where? Though neither one of us wondered this out loud. Sit, sons, was what our father said to us next. Us, our father's sons, we did like our father told. We sat ourselves down, in the middle of the kitchen's floor, right where we were standing, us brothers, we plopped our boy bodies down, down on our hands and knees, and like this we waited for whatever our father was going to say or do to us brothers next. When our father turned back his face so to face his face at us brothers, the look on his man's face told us that he was happy to see us, down like this, down on our hands and knees, us brothers—us, our father's sons—a couple of dirt-loving dogs who liked to get down and get down dirty. It's hot was what our father said to us next, and he held out in his hands, for us brothers to take, a pie that was made out of mud. Blow, our father told us. And we, us brothers, blew. The steam rising up and off of this baked to a crisp-crusted mud, it curled up and around our boy faces—this steam, it became a pair of hands holding us brothers in this place. This is where us brothers like us belong was what these hands whispered up to us. And it was like this, with us brothers down on our hands and knees, and with our mouths wide open, and with our father standing above us, watching over us brothers, his boots skinned thick with mud: like this, we began to eat.

Fish Heads

There was a time when our father, he used to call us brothers Fish Head One and Fish Head Two. Us brothers, we never really knew for sure which of us was which—who was Fish Head One and who was Fish Head Two? In the end, it didn't really matter. When our father called out to one of us brothers, we knew, our father, he was calling out to us two. But one day, us brothers, we each of us got it into our boy heads to wonder: Which of us was who? We both of us believed it, we were the one, that the other brother other than us was the brother second to us. *I'm fish head number one! No I am! Am so! How can you be if I am? We both of us can't be the one!* Like this, back and forth, us brothers, we moved our boy mouths at each other until, after a while, our mouths stopped with all of this back and forth moving, and then those mouthy sounds stopped coming out from our mouths, and when our mouths stopped with this moving what happened then was this: our hands closed up to make, between us brothers, two sets of fists. We each of us that night busted up our knuckles up against each other's face. A piece of my skin, I left it there dangling from one of Brother's front tooths. There was blood on our hands and on the mud in between us—there was blood lipsticked on our lips. But neither one of us brothers wanted to be the brother to give in. We were both of us brothers standing face to face with each other, and with our fists still raised up to our faces, just like our father showed us how to stand when he taught us boys how to fight. We were standing like this, in our fighter's stance, with only our breath funneling up from our lips, when our father stepped out into the back of our backyard. Girls, our father, he called this girl word out—was he calling it out to us boys? Us brothers, the both of us boys hearing this, we both of us unfisted our fists. We turned towards the callering out of that word: Girls. Girls was not a word that we were used to hearing coming out from our father's mouth. Sons and Brothers, Boys and Men, Fish Head One and Fish Head Two—these were the words that we were used to being called when our father wanted us to come here. We stood there and watched, without making a sound, as our father made his way back to where we were both of us brothers standing.

Neither one of us then said a word. We just turned and made a face at each other when we saw our father stop, then turn, then step inside the shed that was our father's. This shed was where our father kept his nuts and his bolts and screws, and his cigar boxes full of rusted, bent-back nails, his buckets and saws, hammers and ropes, and those bottles of his half filled up with whiskey. We could hear our father moving around on the inside of this shed (maybe he was moving things around inside it), but see, we could not see what it was that he was moving around inside. When he stepped back outside from inside this shed, it became clear to us then what it was that he had been doing. In his hand, his right, there was now dangling down from it the curled black claw of a hammer. And in his other hand, his left, which was fisted shut, we could see just the sticking-out tips of a fistful of rusted, bent-back nails. The rust on those nails, the rust, it was shining. We kept watch then as he, our father, he walked back towards us, and then he walked on past us, and what he said to us then was, Fish Heads, come with me. Us brothers, we did what we were told. We turned and we walked with our father, we walked out back into the back of our backyard. We walked like this, boot to boot with our father, until our father stopped and turned back around. We stood, face to face, with our father. We watched our father's face look up. There was no moon to see there in the sky—it was still waiting to rise up from the bottom of our dirty river. What our father was looking at, then, when he lifted up his face, was the creosote-coated telephone pole out back in the back of our yard. This pole, us brothers, we liked to call it, this pole, our backyard fishing pole: it was covered, this pole was, from top to bottom, with the chopped-off heads of fish. These fish, us brothers, we used to fish these fish out of the muddy river than runs its way through this dirty river town. In the end, there were exactly a hundred-and-fifty fish heads hammered and nailed into that pole's creosoted wood. Sometimes, at night, when the moon was good and full—the moon, it was always full—when we lifted up our eyes to take a good look up at these fish, it sometimes looked to us brothers like the fish, the fish heads, open-eyed, open-mouthed, it was like they were singing to us brothers. Each of these fish, each fish head, we gave each one a name. Not one was called Jimmy or John. Jimmy and John, these were my and my brother's names. But we called each other Brother. Our father, when he wasn't calling us Fish Head One and Fish Head Two, our father called out to us brothers, Son. When our father called out to us, Son, us brothers, we both of us knew, we were crossing this river together. And now, standing here like this, we waited to hear what our father—what was he going to say to us brothers next? It was a long few seconds. The sky above the river where the steel mill stretched, shipwrecked in the mud, it was dark and starless. Somewhere, I was sure, the sun was shining. And then, what our father said to us then was: Fish Head One, he said, you can go first. Our father just stood there, staring at us brothers, waiting to see which one of us brothers was going to go first. Us brothers, the two of us, we too just stood there, staring, waiting to see which one of us was going to go first: to see which one of us would be, once and for all, Fish Head One. It was, once again, a long few seconds. The sky, the moon—it was still somewhere at the bottom of the river—it was still waiting to rise up— waiting for one of us brothers to go first. Us brothers, we looked inside each other. There was this look that us brothers, we sometimes looked at each other with. It was a look that actually hurt the eyes of the brother who was doing the looking. Imagine, if you would, that look. Brother was what this look said. Then we both said this word with our mouths. Brother, we both said, at the same time. You can be the one. And then we both said this: It's your turn this time. *But Brother, I went first the first time.* Yes, Brother, but I went first the last time. *No buts.* But really. *But that's all right...* Get the picture? Us brothers, we went back and forth like this, but and but and but, until our father stepped forward and then he stepped in between us brothers. Our father took us brothers both by the hand and he held us so close so that our hands in his hand were facing back to back. And what our father did next was this. He walked with us brothers held by our hands backwards so that it was with our backs that our father, he backed us brothers back up against the bottom of that fish-headed telephone pole. The fish heads staring down upon us brothers, mouths opened wide, eyes marbled moons—those fish, they did not sing for us. This might sting was what our father said to us then. And then he raised back with his hammer, he drove that rusty nail right through the both of us brothers' hands. Us brothers, we didn't wince, or flinch with our bodies, or make with our boy mouths the sound of a brother crying out. Good, Sons, was what our father said to us then. Our father was hammering in the second nail into our hands when our mother stepped out from the inside of our house and into the back of the backyard. Boys, our mother called out to us. Us boys, brothers, with our father in between us, we all three of us turned back our heads towards the sound of that word: boys. We waited to hear what our mother was going to say to us brothers next. It was a long few seconds. The moon, up out of the river, it was just then beginning to rise. You boys be sure to clean up out there before you come back into this house, was what our mother said to us next. Our mother turned back her back. Us brothers, with our father in between us brothers, we turned back to face back each other. Our father raised back his hammer. He lined up that rusted nail.

Boy

We knew this other boy in town who was brother to nobody—
an only child with only a mother and a father and no brother
to call his own. So we took him in as brother. We did not call
him brother though. We called him Boy. Boy was littler than
us brothers. Boy was born years—no, centuries—after we
were born. We were down by the river with our fishing man
father the day that this other brother was born into this
world. This boy, this brother, we were told, was born with
teeth and a full head of hair. What he was not born with, we
discovered, was a tongue. This boy's mouth was a hole in his
face he fed food into. Once in a while, we might hear some
mouthy sounds come grunting out. But for the most part,
Boy was silent. Some of the time we did not even know that
Boy was near, standing close by us brothers, his feet—
flopping inside his father's boots—buried knee-deep in the
river's mud. At times, Boy was more dog than he was a boy.
Boy was a dog who always came whenever we called, to do
whatever we told. Us brothers, we taught Boy more than a

few tricks. We taught Boy how to walk on water. It's true that Boy drowned the first time he walked out. Boy floated face-down down the river. But then he walked upriver back. Back to us brothers. Good dog, we told Boy. We scratched Boy's back. We pulled a bone out from Boy's hand and tossed it to the river. Boy, we told Boy. Go fish. Boy took to that muddy river water like he was part dog, part fish. Boy swam back to the river's muddied bank and flopped down dead right there on the shore. Yes, just like a fish. This boy here, Brother said. He is a keeper, Brother said. If you say so, I said to Brother. And then we chopped off this boy's head.

Where There's Mud Only When It Rains

Us brothers have this cousin of ours who comes once every summer to visit our town to fish. We call him Cousin. Cousin is bigger than us brothers are. He is bigger and he is older too—older by a whole ten years. Old Cousin lives with his mother, our aunt, our father's sister, in a place where there's more dirt than there is water, the kind of a place where there's mud only when it rains. Cousin comes to us to visit our dirty river town and to fish in our muddy river by way of a bus, a big bus with a big gray dog stretched out across its big side. This bus drops him off out by the highway three miles in from our river and also our town. Our father is the one of us who goes and picks Cousin up from where the bus drops him off. But this summer our big cousin comes to town without first calling to tell us he's coming, and so we don't know that it's Cousin coming to visit until we see him walking along the river with a fishing pole sticking out from one hand and a girl who is not his mother being tugged along by the hand that is his other. Hey, Cousin, we call out this cousin word, when we see for sure that it's him. It's been a while, we say, since we saw you last. Last summer, Cousin says, and nods, and then he says, Brothers, this here's my girl. Cousin's girl smiles back at us brothers a kind of a quiet hi there, then she shifts her girl eyes down to look down at our town's ground. Our town's ground is good and muddy after a good night's pouring rain. It's good to see you, we tell Cousin's girl. We give Cousin's girl a good girl looking over. Cousin's girl is good for us brothers to look at. She is pretty-looking in a way that the girls out in our father's shed who are looking out at us brothers from the insides of our father's magazines sometimes look even though some of these girl pictures are crinkled up and finger-smeared with dirt. Cousin's girl looks a bit wrinkled too, her clothes and her face and the way that her hair hangs straight down around her face—this makes us think that it is wet. We could use a shower, Cousin says. Brother says, How about a swim? Brother jerks his chin towards where the river is, where the water is high and good and muddy after the good night's pouring rain. Cousin's girl, when Brother says this, her eyes begin to cry. This girl's cry is the cry of a hundred-thousand birds singing all out of tune. She turns and runs crying back into our house, into the house where all the lights are burned out, inside this house where, behind windows and doors, the sound of this girl's crying is muffled out. Was it something I said? Brother says. Cousin shakes his head no, then he starts in telling us this story about how his girl is afraid of rivers and fish. Cousin, us brothers say this to him, we know how to put an end to a fear like this. And so we both of us brothers go running into our house to go and get this girl out. Inside, Cousin's girl is busy drying her eyes with a towel that is used by our mother's hands to rub our dinner dishes dry. Come with us, we tell this to this girl, and we each of us brothers take hold of this girl by one of her girl arms. When this girl starts to put up a fight, Brother clamps his boy hand over her girl mouth. Like this, with Cousin's girl in between us brothers, we go running back down to the river. The river is moving past us flat and muddy brown. It is a dusty road, this water is, we say, to Cousin's girl. All you have to do is walk across it. The river, we say, it will lift you up. We give Cousin's girl a quick shove and, like this, she begins walking out, she is walking away, she is crossing over to the river's other side. Now look at what you've done, Cousin says to us brothers. She's getting away, he says. She didn't even turn back around to wave goodbye. Wait for me, Cousin calls out after his girl. This girl, she is a runaway horse broke free from a fenced-in stable. Us brothers, we look and we watch Cousin running out into the mud of the river to get back his runaway girl. The muddy river rises up to cut Cousin off at his knees. Cousin keeps going out after his girl, he keeps walking out into the river, until there is only river for us brothers to see. Just like Cousin's girl, Cousin doesn't wave to us brothers goodbye. That night, when the two of us brothers are out fishing for fish, we hook us into a snag. When we free it up, and reel it in, this snag, it turns out to be Cousin's hat. It is the kind of a hat you might see sitting on the head of a cowboy who is sitting on the saddled back of some bucking bronco horse. It is brown and big brimmed, a hat that would be too big to fit our boy beads. And so we toss this too-big hat back into the river. This hat, it floats on top of the water, a bobbing bobber bobbing its headless head, it is floating away from us. Us brothers, we keep on fishing for fish. It doesn't take too long for a fish that looks too much like Cousin not to be Cousin—the walled eyes, the fishy lips—to rise up out of the muddy river to snatch with his hooked mouth this bobbing up and down in the river hat. Fish on! we hear a voice—a girl's—crying this out. It is Cousin's girl's voice. It is Cousin's girl! Cousin's girl is holding on tight to Cousin's fishing pole. It's a big one, this girl, she points this out to us brothers. Us brothers, we take this to mean, Stand back, brothers, and watch how a real girl reels in a fish. So us brothers, we step back and we watch this girl set back the barbed hook. When she does, when she pulls back on this bent-over fishing pole, the big silver hook pulls loose like a busted off tooth. The see-through fishing line dangles slack from the tip of this girl's pole. This fish, it is a running away horse-fish running free and running wild across this wide open field that, once upon a time ago—centuries ago—it used to be called not the river but the sea.

The Singing Fish: Revisited

Girl held out to us brothers to take her hand. There were these rivers there in the palm of Girl's hand, there in the hubs of her knuckles—there were these rivers there filled with singing fish. It was these singing fish singing that lured us brothers to dive hands-first in. These fishes' song, it was a rusty hook that hooked its barbs into us brothers—it dug its hooks into our muddy brother hearts. When Girl gave us brothers her hand and told us to take it, when she told us to look inside that rivery place, we looked to see if we might see down to the bottom of that river so that we might see those singing fish singing up. We looked and we looked but we could not see all the way down, so we waded in slow from the river's muddy bank. We waded in slow, and then we let the water rise up from that singing place below. We did not fight it. We let ourselves get reeled in by the singing of those fish. Our boy mouths, we puckered them up to swallow down inside us the sound of those fish-singing songs. The moon too—the moon, it was a fish eye shining down all moony-eyed from this fish-headed sky—the moon, it was singing now to us brothers too. We flopped our mud-scaled bodies down upon the mud that was made by this river. These fish here, we heard Girl say. These boys here. These brothers are a couple of keepers. We flexed our boy muscles, shook our fish tails, we flared out our hairs until they hackled up stiff from the backs of our stubble-scaled necks. Then, we waited for what we knew was bound to happen to us brothers next. It was a long few seconds. The skies above the river where the steel mill stood shipwrecked—it was dark and quiet. Somewhere, I knew for sure, the sun was shining. And so, us brothers, here in this river darkness, we started singing. We kept on singing. We kept on singing, then we kept on singing louder, when we saw Girl fish out with her other hand a mud-dripping knife that she raised up over our boy heads. Us brothers, we opened up our mouths. We sang like singing fish. We sang and we sang until Girl brought her mud hand down over the tops of us brothers and chopped off our boy heads.

Keepers

This fish was the biggest of the big-lipped fishes that us brothers ever fished from out of this fishy river that runs through this fishy river town—this fish, it was so big it was a fish too big for us brothers to lay it sideways or frontways down into our mud-rusty buckets—this fish, it was a fish too big for us boys to lift it up from the mud it was laying on—it was a fish too big even for us brothers to drag it back up from the muddy banks of our muddy river back to the back of our house. And so what us brothers did with this fish was, we let it lay there, there at the edge of the river, where it was breathing in this mud that was now this fish's new riverless river—it was now its new muddy bed. But what are we gonna do with a fish this big? Brother wanted to know this. I too didn't know what we'd do with a fish this big, so what I said was, Brother, I don't know what. We could, Brother said, cut this fish up into littler fish pieces that would be small enough to fit them into our buckets. So us brothers, the both of us, we fished out our fishing knives from out of our trouser pockets. But just as us brothers were about to get down onto our hands and knees to begin the cutting up of this big fish into littler pieces of this fish, this big fish opened up its big-lipped mouth. When us brothers saw this, when this big fish's mouth opened so wide open we could see all the way down inside it, what we thought was: this big fish is opening up its big-lipped mouth and is going to swallow us brothers up. But what this big fish did, when it opened up its mouth—no, it didn't swallow us brothers up. This fish did not want to eat either one of us brothers up. What it wanted, why this big fish opened up its mouth was: it wanted to talk. There were these sounds coming up out of this fish's mouth that was like the sound that words sometimes make when you say them inside of a cave. But it wasn't really this big fish that was the fish making this sound. When this fish opened its mouth—to do what, us brothers, we did not know—what happened was this: a bunch of other fish, fish much littler and little enough to fit inside this bigger fish's insides, these much smaller fish started walking out of this bigger fish's mouth. There were ten of these littler fish in all on the inside of this much bigger fish. These ten much littler fish, if you could take a look at these fish, you would see and say it, too, that they weren't all that little: these fish, they were pretty big fish. They were fish that you could even call good-sized fish, though they were still little enough to fit into our buckets and into our mother's skillet, though lately, with this burnt-bottomed skillet, our mother hadn't been doing much cooking. Us brothers knew it, we could carry these littler fish up and back to our house, back to our backyard, where we'd gut and we'd clean and we'd cut off these littler fishes' heads and then nail them, these heads, with the eyes of them still staring out at us brothers, we would hammer those fish heads into our fish-headed telephone pole, what us brothers called our backyard fishing pole, that was out back in the back of our backyard. We could already picture this in our boy heads: these ten new fish heads still glistening, nailed to the telephone pole's creosoted wood, their fish mouths opened wide with singing. We were already beginning to forget about that other fish, that big fish, that fish so big we didn't know what to do with this fish. We were brothers by now busy picturing these ten new fish heads up on our backyard fishing pole, us brothers whispering names to each other—new names to give to these newest of ten fish heads. One of us brothers had just finished mouthing the sound Samson when one of these little fish opened up its mouth to speak. You boys can have the ten of us, this one littler fish said to us brothers, but for us ten littler fish, it said, we ask that you give our father—and here this fish pointed with its fin towards the big fish it had moments ago come marching out of—we insist that you throw our father back into the river, back to where he came. Us brothers gave this fish that was doing this talking the look that we liked to give each other: this look that was a dare between us brothers—it was a look that said, All right, Brother, but I get to go first. But first, us brothers said, right back at this fish, we'd like to ask your father this. We all of us, brothers and fish alike, looked over to where the big fish was laying, down in the mud, looking, it looked like to us, like it was a fish already dead. If we throw *your* father back into the river, would you tell him to take a message to *our* father? A message to *your* father? the littler fish said to this. Yes, *our* father, the both of us brothers said, and we bobbered our boy heads together. Tell your father what? the fish said. Tell him, we said, say to our father what we sometimes say to fish too small for us to bucket and gut and clean, we said. Come back, is what we say, when you grow up to be good and big. We stuck out our hands then to shake the fin of this fish who was doing the talking. When we shook this fish's fin, it was like shaking the hand of a brother. Good, Brother, we said to this fish. Together, the two of us brothers with the help of these ten littler fish, we inch by inch dragged and pushed and kicked and flipped that big fish back to where it came. Once this big fish had enough water beneath it to hold its belly up to float, to let the river once again fill and to river in through its gills, we watched this too-big fish turn back into muddy water. Say hello to our father, us brothers hollered out to this fish. *I am your father* is what we heard a voice from the river say, a rivery echo that rose up, or maybe it even crossed through mud and water, to bring itself up to us. Us brothers, we both looked across at each other, then we turned back to face the fish who were soon to become our brothers. Keepers, we called these fish. And then we fished out the knives hiding inside our trouser pockets and we cut off each of these ten fish heads.

Guts

Our father baits his fishing hooks with mud.

Us brothers, we watch our father do this hooking, dipping his mud-covered hand into his rusted bucket of mud.

He casts his muddy hooks out into the night's dark— the river's darker waters.

We wait.

Patience, our father says.

We wait some more.

Fish on, our father cries.

Our father pulls back on his rod.

You gotta set the hook hard, like you mean it, he tells us. Show those fish who's boss.

He reels in line. His knuckles shine white from under his mud-gloved skin.

Our father's fishing pole is alive with this big fish's underwater tugging.

Keep the rod's tip up, our father tells us.

Slack, our father warns, is bad.

Tension, our father says.

Tension is good.

We see the fish rise up out of the muddy waters.

The fish's eyes are moons rising up into the river's mud-darkened skies.

Our father rips the hook from this fish's mouth, then pitches this fish into the bucket.

Where there's one fish, he says.

He doesn't say anything else.

He dunks his hand once again in the muddy bucket of mud.

He baits and makes his hook more muddy with mud.

We watch him cast out his line into the muddy dark.

We hear the sinker sink.

Hear it go *ker-plink, ker-plunk.*

Hear it.

See it sinking.

It sinks.

There is a current here. There is an undertow here that will tug you down to the river's muddy bottom.

The river's motto is, Sink or swim.

It is dark and muddy down here at the edge of this muddy river.

Our father waits for something to happen.

Us brothers wait for something to happen.

The stars above us shine.

Fish on, our father says.

Our father hands us brothers the butt of his rod.

It is cork-gripped.

It is alive with a fish tugging at its tip.

We know it is there even though we cannot see it.

This fish.

We take turns reeling in.

We take turns baiting the hook.

We take turns setting the hook.

One by one, the fish come in.

One.

Two.

Three.

Four.

The bucket slowly fills up to its muddy rim.

So many moons glowing unseen underneath the river's muddy water.

We take the fish home.

Here, our father says, and hands each of us brothers a knife.

Now it's time to clean.

We do not like that word, clean.

Us brothers like dirt, like mud, like dirty.

Our father says for us to, Gut them good.

Gut is better.

Gut is better than clean.

Our father shows us how to do the gutting right.

The knife feels good in us brothers' hands.

I can speak for my brother.

We are brothers.

We are each other's voice inside our own heads.

Our father takes a fish out of the bucket.

This fish, it is not dead.

This fish is still alive and kicking in our father's muddy hands.

The muddied water in the bucket goes splish, it goes splash.

We watch our father do this thing with his hands.

We know what our father can do with his hands.

Watch this, he says.

Our father takes this kicking fish and he lays this fish down, on its one-eyed side, on a scrap piece of wood. We watch our father take his hammer and a rusty, bent-back nail and he nails this nail through this fish's tail. This fish kicks, it stiffens, it shakes its fish head. Its gill-plates flitch open, switchblade-quick, so that we see inside it: red.

We see our father set down his hammer and take up his knife. This is a thing he is good at. See him stick the pointy tip of the knife blade into the fish's white underbelly, see his big-knuckled hand give a quick push in until the knife slips in through a slit in the scaly skin and guts, muddy-colored, come slushing out.

There is this sound the fish makes when our father's knife disappears a quarter of the way into the fish's white belly. It is a sound that sounds as though the fish is saying, Shish.

Or, Shush.

Listen.

Look.

Our father cups the whole of his hand up inside the gutty innards of this fish and swipes out this inside mess in one quick swoop. Intestines, stomach, liver, heart. Whatever else this muck is called that makes up the insides here on the inside of these fish.

Our father takes these guts and dumps them out into this other bucket that sits next to the bucket with the other fish inside of it, where every once in a while a fish will flare and flick its back fin up against the bucket's metal insides, to say what, to us brothers, we don't for sure know. If I had to guess, I'd guess that it was saying:

I know that I am about to be gutted.

I know that I am about to breathe my last breath.

I do not feel sorry for these fish.

These fish are not my brothers.

My brother, who I call just plain Brother, says to us then, Look at that fish.

We look.

He points to the bucket with the fish swimming inside it.

He points to this one fish looking up at us.

What, we say.

It's looking at us, Brother says.

What else has it got to look at, our father says to this.

Brother doesn't say a thing to that.

He knows better than to say a thing back.

Our father gets back to the gutting of these fish. He sticks the nozzle-end of the backyard garden hose up inside the belly of the fish. He holds the fish up. There's a fountainy stream of water shooting out of its fish mouth. Us brothers know that this is meant to make us laugh.

We laugh.

Our father puts back down this fish.

Look.

This fish has got no guts inside it.

It is dead.

Look again.

It is not dead.

We see its fish gills fan out as if it just took in a big gulping breath of unfresh, unfishy, otherworldly air.

There is something, too, about this fish's looking-up-at-us fish eye that makes us brothers believe that, this fish, it is alive.

I say these words to our father who is looking around for his hammer again, who isn't looking down at this fish.

Brother says these words, too.

Us brothers sometimes have this thing between us. Sometimes we say what it is the other brother is or has been thinking.

Our father lets us brothers know to think, to look, again.

It's dead, our father says. It's dead and it's not going nowhere but in our guts.

I can't help but picture fish, swimming around inside our bellies, looking for a way to get out.

I open up my mouth.

Nothing comes out.

Okay, now, we hear our father say to us brothers. Who's going first?

We both turn toward our father. Up until now I have forgotten about the knife hanging down from my right hand. It was just there, this thing in my grip—a sixth finger.

Now it is an ax.

It is heavy.

It is big.

It could chop off a grown man's head.

We look at our father.

We both say, to each of us other's brother, our two voices becoming one:

Brother, you can go first.

We both say, No. It's okay. You go, Brother. No, you go. No, you go.

We go back and forth, like this, until our father steps in between us. He takes me by the back of the neck and pushes his weight down over me until I drop to my knees in front of the buckets—one bucket of mud, one of guts, the other bucket filled with fish.

Get gutting is what I hear our father say.

I look back up at Brother. He is looking down at me. Us brothers have got these looks between us that we like to give each other when it is not possible to say what it is that we would really like to say.

I say, to our father, Which one of these fish has got my name written on it?

He points to the biggest fish in the bucket. I can see that it's still alive and kicking its fins, scuffing its scales against the bucket's rusted steel. It looks like the kind of a fish that, when it was born, it was born with a mouth full of teeth.

I reach for the bucket.

I reach in and fish my hands around for this fish.

I take hold of this fish. It is alive in my hands. It is alive, I know, though not for long, not as long as I've got this knife.

It is in my hands now.

This knife.

This fish.

I know what I have to do.

I pick the fish up out of the bucket, hold it up above my head. It is as big, I can see, as the sky is wide. It is, to me, the way that this fish feels in my hands, bigger than me.

Then, this fish, it kicks and swims out of my grip, this fish, it arcs out into the sky, and then it lands on the backyard ground with a heavy flopping sound. This is the sound, I imagine, of the fish's guts getting slopped around inside it.

This fish, the way it skirts across the backyard dirt, it doesn't seem to be hurt. It makes like it can swim without water. The way it flips its fins, flaps its tail, it makes me believe it.

It is swimming.

I am telling you that this fish, it is swimming across the earth.

I kick over the bucket of fish in my running after this fish. All the rest of the fish in this bucket spill out onto the grass.

The grass is a deep and deeply-colored green: lots of rain. It has been one of those summers.

All the fish, even those already dead and stiff, they start to swim away.

We run, us brothers, our father with us, after the getting-away fish.

Get them, I hear our father's voice say, before they get down to the river.

These fish are fish on the run.

These are fish that can walk on water, that can swim across grass and mud.

Us brothers run with our knives in our hands.

Our father is running with his hammer.

Come back here!

You can't do that!

We're gonna kill you!

This is us talking to the fish.

Up above us the moon is watching. It is looking down upon us brothers with this grin that is digging a river across its face. You can actually hear the moon's laughter.

This moony laughter that I think is the moon's, it is actually the fish.

It is the fish and not the moon.

Or it is both the fish and the moon's laughter that we hear laughing down at us.

We do not think that this is funny.

You, do not think that this is funny.

Remember the knives.

Do not forget about the hammer in our father's fist.

We know how to use these things.

We've got the guts to use them.

We know how to make a knife sing.

It is a song that we sing along with.

I am mad with this singing.

I am happy to be alive and running after these running-away fish.

We catch up to the fish.

We catch these fish.

I get my hands on the biggest one.

I take the hammer from our father.

I nail this fish's tail into wood.

Then I take the knife. I take the knife and head-first I cut off, I saw off, I chop off, this fish's head first.

I leave the guts for later.

I save what's inside for last.

This fish's head is all mine.

This fish head, I give the head a name.

I begin at the beginning.

Adam, I say.

Adam is the first name that comes into my head.

So I name this fish, this fish head, Adam.

This fish, I can tell, it is a boy fish.

I know this to be true because I am a boy, too.

I take this fish head Adam, I take the hammer, and then I nail him into the fish-headed telephone pole out back in the back of our yard.

And what about the fish's body?

The body is another story.

I hammer in this fish head so that it is a fish head that is facing east.

East is where the river is.

Say hello, Adam, I say this to this fish.

I whisper this into where I imagine the fish's ear is.

I raise back the hammer again.

This, I whisper this.

I sing this whisper into this fish head.

This here is your new home.

Boy: Revisited

We see Boy. Boy is down by the river—us brothers, we can see this—but what Boy is doing, down by the river, us boys, this, we cannot see. What we can see is Boy's back: it is facing us brothers, and Boy's face, his eyes, his nose, his mouth with no tongue inside it—it is just a hole that Boy puts food into, where no words ever come out—Boy's face, it is away from us brothers facing into the dark. But Boy's face, even though we cannot see it, us brothers know, because we know Boy, that his face—it is raised to gaze up at the moon. That face that is gazing down from the moon, that moon face, even a blind boy could see it. Or maybe a boy born blind, marbly-eyed, maybe a blind boy could see the moon's face so much better. All we know for sure is what our own eyes tell us to see. Us brothers, our eyes, we believe that our eyes see more than most eyes see. This is just a thing we have come to believe. And here is one more thing about us brothers believing: we believe we don't have to see a thing to believe it to be true. But us brothers, we know this other thing is true, too: that most people—are you like most people?—these people, they need to see a thing in order to believe it. It's because of this, us brothers, what we say to this is: look. See Boy. See Boy with his back to us brothers. Boy's shadow, it is made to be bigger than Boy is, it is made big by the way the moon's face shines its moonlight down onto Boy's face. Boy, see Boy's shadow—it is floating face-down on top of the river. It is a bridge for us brothers to walk our boots across. See Boy, the body, not the shadow of Boy, reach down with his boy hand down into the mud that he is standing in, and see that he is up from the mud picking something up into his boy hand. Us brothers, we can't see it, what this something is that Boy has reached down to pick up into his hand, though we can see that it's something that Boy is getting ready to throw. See Boy reach back with his hand that just a moment ago was the hand that was reaching down into the mud, and watch Boy throw whatever it is that he is holding in this hand out into the river's dark. Listen: this thing that Boy has just thrown, when it hits the water, it doesn't make a sound. Whatever it was that Boy was in his hand a moment ago holding, whatever it is that Boy was throwing into the river's dark, when it meets the river's muddy water, it doesn't make a splash. No, there is only that sound of us brothers breathing when we run ourselves down to the river so that we can with our eyes better see. When Boy sees that it's us brothers who are running down to the river, he turns and then he turns back around. It's only us is what Boy's body is saying to us. We've been watching, is what us brothers, with our boy mouths, we mouth these words to Boy. We tell Boy we saw him, Boy, we saw you picking something up, though picking up what, and Boy throwing that whatever something out into the river's dark: this, us brothers, this we do not know. We cannot fill in this blank with our knowing. Boy points with one hand up to the moon floating fish-belly-white above us, but it's Boy's other hand that we make our eyes see. It's the hand of Boy that is reaching back down towards the mud, and it's up from the mud picking some other thing up. What this other thing is, it comes clear to us brothers what it is, when the moon's moonlight lights up for us what this something other is. What this something other is is, it is a picture, it is a photograph. But no, look again: it is not a picture of us. What it is, this picture, is it's a picture of Boy.

It's a picture of Boy back when Boy was a boy littler than the boy he is now. In this picture of Boy, Boy is just a baby—he is just a baby Boy—and in this picture, Boy's mouth, it is a hole with a whole lot of light shining out. Boy's mouth, that hole on Boy's face with no tongue inside it, it is a moon in this picture, it is a lighthouse light—it is the marbled eye of a fish. And in this picture, standing on both sides of Boy, with a hand holding on to each of Boy's hands, there is with him in this picture a man and a woman who are, we can see, a father and a mother to this boy Boy. This is the boy that, us brothers, we do not call him Brother. No, this boy, us brothers, we call him Boy. There are other pictures like this picture, too—pictures stuck picture-side-up in the mud at Boy's feet. But it is Boy's hand that we, us brothers, with our seeing eyes, this is what we are staring at. Boy's hand might as well be, to us brothers, a star that has just now fallen. This is what we see. When Boy reaches back with his stone-throwing hand to do to this picture whatever it is he is wishing to do to it: to throw it, this picture, into the river, out into that rivery dark (yes, this is what it seems to be what Boy is going to do). But instead, what happens is, this picture, and the other pictures like this picture, this picture, it does not do like what a stone would do if a stone was skipped, if it was thrown, out into the river. This picture, in the wind that blows in with the river, it blows this picture right back into Boy's face. See Boy with his hands right now empty-handed, he is standing facing the river, and with his boy head he is shaking, he is hanging his head down low. What this, what his head, is saying to us brothers is that Boy does not know what to do. Us brothers though, we know exactly what it is Boy should be doing. We drop down on our hands and knees, down into the mud, here at Boy's feet, and we pick up, one by one, all of these fallen down pictures. When we're done, up from the mud, picking up all of these pictures, we say to Boy: Boy, come with us. We take Boy by the hand, down along the river, down to where there is this bridge down here that crosses out across the river. It's a bridge where no one is supposed to ever walk. Us brothers, we walk with Boy out to where this bridge is, and we walk out, above the water, half the way across. Here, we say. These are for you. And then we hand over into Boy's hand all of the pictures that us brothers have been holding in our hands. Now open up your hands, we say to Boy. Boy, we tell Boy, it is time to let this all go. Boy nods, because Boy is the good boy that he is. He listens to what us brothers have to tell him, and he lets the pictures in his hands all go. Fall, these pictures, they all fall floating down into the muddy river below. If you could see what the eyes of us brothers did see—this is what we would want you to see. See a hundred boy faces of Boy, open-eyed, open-mouthed, a hundred of these boys floating face-down on down the river. Our hands in our pockets, we cannot help but fish them out to wave to these boys goodbye. But when we look closer we see, in Boy's hand, we see, there is still this one picture left—it is a picture that Boy cannot let go. This picture, this one picture that is left, this picture that this boy Boy has not yet let go of, we see it: it is a picture of us. This picture is a picture of us brothers, from back on the day when we first gazed our eyes upon this boy Boy—that day when us brothers, we taught Boy to walk on water. We taught Boy to believe. I can still picture it, the way Boy floated face-down down the river. Like most boys, Boy didn't believe enough. But then Boy came back a second time. Just like that, he walked up the river back—back to us brothers. Good dog,

Boy, us brothers, we said this to Boy. That was the day when Brother turned to me after Boy came walking up the river back to us and what Brother said was, he said, to me, This boy here, Brother said, he is a keeper. If you say so, I said to this, and I reached into my trouser pocket, I fished out the fishing knife that was hiding inside there. Brother took Boy by the skin of Boy's neck. Here, Brother said, stay right here, and he stood Boy up in the moonlight. That knife in my hand shined its own light into Boy's ear. I am not imagining this when I say that what Boy heard inside of his ear—it was singing. And when I cut off his boy head, Boy did not wince, or flinch with his body, or make with his boy mouth the sound of a brother crying out. Good, Brother, I said. Hey, Boys. We now hear the sound of this word—a voice, a sound—calling out to us: boys. Us brothers, we turn back around to face the sound of this word: boys. We look around in that dark above the river to see who it is that is calling out to us—not as brothers, but as boys. This sound, the way that the "s" sound in that word *boys* floats in that space above the river: it hangs in the air as if the air is a river and it, this sound, is a fish, a picture of a fish, floating on this river's top.

This sound, the voice of it, it sounds too much like the way our father used to sound when he used to call out to us to come home to eat. In the river's dark, we see our father, across the water, he is walking back towards us. Us brothers—us, our father's sons—we wait to hear what it is that our father is going to say to us next. It is a long few seconds. The sky above the river where the steel mill sits shipwrecked, it is starless and quiet. Somewhere, I am sure, the sun is shining. I believe, our father says to us, and he reaches out towards us. This picture, he says, it belongs to me. He takes this picture from out of our hands and he looks into the faces of us. Then he turns with the picture still in his hand and he walks back out across the river, back to the river's other side, walking and walking and walking on, until he is nothing but the sound that the river sometimes makes when a stone is skipped across it.

The Fish That Walked On Water

Only us brothers were there, that night, down by the river, that night, to see the fish that walked on water. What's that there? Brother said, and the both of us brothers, we both stood up from where we were sitting, down by and down on the river's muddy shore, down where river and dirt kiss to make mud, so that the both of us brothers could see what there was for us to see. From down here, looking up, us brothers, the both of us did see. See on the water? Brother said, to me, to us, to the river, and the mud, and the moon up in the sky. What is it? Is it a buoy? Brother wondered. I stood up and I looked across the muddy river water, and what I saw moving across the water's top, this was no buoy. Buoys don't move, was what I said to Brother. I said this to the river, too, and to the mud, too, and to the moon, too. But they do rock, buoys rock, Brother said right back to what I had just said. Back and forth, Brother said, and when I turned to look back at Brother, I saw Brother, he was making like he was a buoy, bobbing back and forth in the river's wake. It could be a boat,

I said, and with my hands I made my hands into handmade binoculars for my eyes to better see through. It could be, Brother agreed, though he was still making like he was a buoy. Let's wait and see if it'll come closer. We waited for whatever it was to come closer. It did, after a while, come closer. And when it did, when it was close enough for us to see what it was, moving across, on top of the water, it was clear to the both of us brothers just what it was. A fish, a fish! us brothers both of us sang this out. We sang it out so loud that even the moon looked down to see what all our singing was about. A fish that walks on water! I said this to the river, though my voice, now, when I heard it say these words, it was singing all by itself. I looked over at Brother. Why wasn't Brother singing with Brother? was what I wanted to know. But Brother wasn't singing and Brother wasn't saying anything but *but*, *but*, because, for a moment, Brother was, with his mud brain, Brother was too busy thinking, *can't*. But fish can't walk on water, was what Brother said. Yes, Brother actually said this. Then he said this too: Fish swim in, inside, beneath, the river. This was what Brother's brain thinking made Brother's mouth open up and say. I shook my head at

Brother. Then I gave Brother this look. If I had a hammer in my hand, was what this look said. Only the river knows what I might have done to Brother. No, if I had a hammer, us brothers, we both know—you know it too if you've been listening along with us—we all know what I would have done. But instead, I put my words to work. Look at this fish go! I said. Go, fish, go! Go, go! And I kept on saying this, these words, Go, fish, go! Go, fish, go! Go, fish, go! over and over, with my fist raised to the sky, hammering away at the moon, and I kept on saying these words, and I kept on hammering away at the moon, I kept hammering away at Brother, until Brother sang these words with me too. Both of us brothers were now singing this song together. We were the both of us brothers ripping off hunks from the moon with the muddy-clawed hammers that were our fists. And that fish that walked on water, when this fish heard the sounds of us brothers singing from the river's muddy shore, this fish turned its fish head towards the sound that us brothers were making, and what this fish did was, this fish walked across that river's muddy water, over to us brothers, and what it said to us then was, What are you two looking at? Then:

What are you two boys waiting for? And when this fish said this, what this fish did was it held out its fins for us brothers to take hold. You want to go for a walk on water? was what this fish said to us next. Yes, we did. Yes, us brothers, we nodded yes with our boy heads. We took hold of this fish's fins and when we did this, this fish took hold of us brothers and it took us out for a walk, walking out across that river's muddy water. Us brothers, we were two dogs to this one fish. We wanted to run. Whoa, now, this fish told us. Take it slow. Good, this fish then said. That's right. Good. One foot, and then the other foot, was what this fish was teaching us. Breathe in, breathe out. Good, brothers, this fish said, to us brothers. Now, this fish told us. Now, it said, I'm going to let go. This fish did like this fish told. Us brothers, we were let go. Now walk, was what this fish told us brothers to do. And so we did like this fish told. We walked. Out on the river's water, across the muddy water, us brothers, we walked. And we did not look back, we did not stop walking—not until we heard a sound that sounded like the sound the river sometimes makes when a stone is skipped across it. When we heard that sound, we stopped and we turned back to see what it was. It was the fish that walked on water. Go, boys, go! this fish, it shouted this out to us. And don't you boys come back. Go fish some other waters, this fish, it told this to us brothers. Us brothers, we turned back around. And we walked back across, on top of, that muddy river water. We did not stop walking until we stood toe to tail to this fish. We looked this fish straight in its fish eye. And we both knew what it was that we had to do to this fish. Brother, I said to Brother. You can go first. Brother did like I told. Brother took hold of this fish's fin. Then we walked with this fish, back to our house, to take it to its new home. We walked this fish back to the fish-headed telephone pole that was out back in the back of our backyard. I handed over to Brother the hammer, and a handful of rusty, bent-back nails. Then I held this fish's fin up against the pole's wood. Brother did all the rest. This might sting, Brother said to this fish, and then he raised back that hammer, he drove that rusted nail right through this fish's fin. This fish, it didn't even wince, or flinch with its body, or make with its fish mouth the sound of a fish crying out. Good, fish, us brothers said to this fish. Brother was hammering in a second nail into this fish's other fin when our father stepped out back into the back of the yard. Sons, our father said. We turned back toward the sound of our father. We waited to hear what it was that our father was going to say to us brothers next. It was a long few seconds. The sky above the river where the steel mill stood shipwrecked in the mud, it was dark and quiet. Somewhere, I was sure, the sun was shining. You boys remember to wash up before you come back in, our father said. Our father turned back his back. Us brothers turned back to face back with this fish. Brother raised back with the hammer. He lined up that rusted nail.

Mud Soup

There is mud, us brothers know, that will not let you walk across it. When you try to walk across this mud, this mud, it swallows you up. It is like the river's water, but only thicker. Us brothers, we know boys who've gotten themselves sucked down to the neck in this kind of mud. Some boys, they call this mud quick mud. This mud, it makes soup out of boys not like us brothers—boys who don't know how to walk on water, boys who don't know how to walk across mud. Those boys are the kind of a boy who, when he sees this kind of mud, he does not see that this mud, it is the kind of mud that will not hold a boy up. One time, us brothers, we got it going on inside our boy heads to wonder: How deep into the earth did this kind of mud go? And so we dove down, headfirst, down into this mud. We dug and we dug and we muddied our way down, and downer, into the muddy earth—but after three days of us doing this, we did not get down to this mud's muddy bottom. So we dug back up, and we flapped with our arms back up, until we had muddied our way back up to the top of all this mud. When we got back up, us brothers, we were covered up with mud. Girl was up there waiting for us when we got back up. We told Girl our story, that there was no end to this mud that we could see—that we could not get down to this mud's muddy bottom. But Girl didn't believe us. Girl said we were making it up. Then Girl stepped with both of her girl feet into this bottomless mud. Us brothers, we watched Girl lift up the cottony hem of her girl dress. The mud reached up just barely to kiss Girl's knees. Girl's knees, they are the kind of knees that make us brothers want to stay forever kneeling. When Girl stepped into this mud, it was like dipping the oar of a rower's boat into a muddy puddle. It's true, Girl was that big. Girl was so big, us brothers, we climbed our way up the side of her mud-barked body as if she were a tree. This tree, we knew, we would never get up to the top. Something would stop us—the moon, the stars. Some passing by bird or aeroplane would get in our climbing way. The moon rising up rose, but it stopped rising up when it got all tangled up in Girl's hair. Girl didn't hardly notice the moon getting itself all tangled up in Girl's hair. Girl thought the moon was just a knot of hair that the wind had twisted up. Girl walked around for a month with the moon sitting on the top of her girl head. It wasn't until the thirty-third day of this did Girl reach up with her hand and Girl flicked the moon back into its orbit. The moon rose like a balloon running away from the hand of a little girl who wanted to know what it would be like to see this balloon rise up and up until, in the sun's heat, it would get so close up, it would get so heated up, that it would break. It's true that the moon was rising up and away from the hand, from the head, of a girl, Girl, who did not realize that the moon could actually break. When the moon in its rising up, when the moon got too up close to the sun, it was too late for us brothers to stop it from breaking. In the sun's molten light, in this blast furnace fire, the moon, it shattered into a billion pieces. Each broken piece became a star.

Boy: Revisited

Boy wants Girl.

Boy wants Girl but Brother says no to this boy's wanting.

Girl is ours, Brother says.

Girl, we made Girl.

We made Girl, we say, the same way we made Boy.

This is what we did.

Picture this.

Picture us brothers.

Picture us brothers standing down by the river's edge.

See us brothers.

We drop down onto our hands and knees.

Here, where river water meets dirt, we make mud.

We make Girl.

We start at the bottom and make our way up.

Girl's knees are especially muddy.

Girl's knees make us brothers want to remain forever in the mud kneeling.

Us brothers, we can barely stand it to look Girl straight in the eye.

Girl is that beautiful.

Girl is that muddy.

Girl's eyes and Girl's hair and Girl's skin too—all the color of mud.

Us brothers, we love mud.

Mud, us brothers, we can never get enough of mud.

But, but, Boy starts to stutter back to us brothers.

But nothing, us brothers cut Boy off before he can begin to begin what it is he is wanting to say.

Listen, we say.

We tell Boy what we just told you.

We love mud.

Mud, us brothers, we can never get enough of mud.

Girl is pure mud.

Girl, Brother tells Boy, Girl is even better than mud.

When Brother says this, I give Brother this look.

Us brothers, we've got this look that we sometimes like to look at each other with. It's the kind of a look that actually hurts the face of the brother who is doing the looking.

Imagine that look.

Look, we say this word to Boy.

Boy, just like you, Boy.

We say these words to Boy too.

Girl began as mud, too.

Girl began as mud, we say, but Girl became a girl when we gave Girl her name.

We named Girl Girl because that's what she looked like: girl.

Girl, we said.

And the name stuck like a stick stuck into the mud.

We took a stick and we wrote Girl's name into the mud down by the edge of the muddy river.

G-I-R-L.

Girl looked good looking up at us brothers up from down in the mud.

But, Boy says that word again.

Boy says, But you already told me this story.

Boy tells us brothers, I already know all about mud and Girl.

I already know, Boy says, all about how Girl began as mud.

Boy says, I already know all about how it was you brothers who made Girl up from the mud rise up.

Tell me something new, this boy says to us brothers.

Tell me something I don't already know, is what Boy wants us brothers to tell him.

Then Boy says something that Boy shouldn't be saying.

But I'm like a brother, is what Boy says.

But what Boy doesn't know is, Boy knows nothing about what it takes to be a brother—what it takes to be one of us.

Boy brings his face in closer to us brothers.

Then Boy says, breathing his breath up into our faces:

I am one of you.

Us brothers, the both of us, our hands close up into fists.

Us brothers, the both of us brothers, we shake our heads at this boy: no.

There is no *like*, we tell Boy.

There is no like when it comes down to being a brother, we say.

You are, we say, or you aren't.

Just because, we say, you're a boy, we say.

We look down at Boy. We shake our boy heads at Boy.

There is more to being a brother, Brother says.

There is more to becoming a brother, us brothers say, than just being a boy.

Boy nods his boy head as if to tell us brothers that he gets what it is we are saying.

But Boy, I'll tell you right now. But I don't say this. Boy does not know the beginning of what we are saying.

Teach me, Boy says. Tell me what I've got to do to become more than just a boy.

So we do.

Maybe, us brothers, the both of us get it into our heads thinking: maybe this boy is a keeper.

Look.

Look at us brothers looking at each other with that between-us-brothers kind of a look.

If you say so, we say so to Boy.

Brother takes a stick—it's the same stick that we used to write Girl's name into the mud with—and Brother throws this stick as far as a brother can throw a stick like this out into the river.

Brother throws this stick all the way across the river, all the way over to the river's other side.

Boy, us brothers say to Boy.

Go fetch.

Boy does like he is told.

Boy takes to that muddy river like he is part dog, part fish.

Boy fetches that stick and then he swims back to the river's muddy shore.

Boy flops down in the mud here at the river's edge.

Like a dog.

Boy is a dog scratching his own dog back, or a fish trying to spit loose a hook that is hooked into his fish mouth.

Good dog, Brother says to Boy.

Good fish, I say to this.

It's true that Boy was born into this world with a head full of mud hair, with a mouth full of made out of mud teeth.

What Boy was not born with, we discovered, was a tongue inside his boy mouth.

This boy's mouth was a hole in his boy face that he fed food into.

In the beginning, Boy could not speak.

It was us brothers who taught this boy how to talk.

We pointed at Girl and we said that word, girl.

We said that word girl but not the way that other boys say it.

We said girl the way girl was meant to be said: with twelve r's, thirteen u's, and twenty-thousand l's at the end of girl, stretching across the earth.

When Boy heard us brothers say that word girl, Boy grunted.

Boy howled.

Boy pointed at what he wanted to say: mud, river, moon, girl.

But still he could not speak.

So one night, us brothers, we took this boy Boy by his boy hand and we told him to drop down, onto his knees, down into the mud.

Boy did like we told.

If it looks to you like what we were doing with Boy was trying to get him to drop down to his knees to say a prayer, look again.

What we told Boy to do was, with his hands, was to take up into his hands a handful of mud, and then we told this boy to eat.

We told Boy not to stop with this eating until the moon disappeared from the night's sky.

In the morning, when we told Boy to open up his mouth, he had a tongue inside there that was made out of mud.

When Boy opened up his mouth, that word girl, it came singing out.

Boy hasn't stopped singing that word girl, he hasn't stopped singing about Girl, ever since.

He hasn't stopped barking up the legs of us brothers, asking us, telling us that he, Boy, wants Girl.

Boy, we tell Boy.

Girl is ours.

We both of us brothers scratch Boy's back.

We pull a bone from the back of Boy's hand and sling it into the river.

Boy, we tell Boy. Go fish.

Once again, Boy does what he is told.

Us brothers, remember, a brother to us is what Boy wants himself to one day be.

When Boy fetches the bone from the back of his own hand back from this river's other side, when he flops his boy body down in the mud here at the river's edge, what Boy says, when he gazes up at us brothers is, Now am I a brother?

What Boy begs from us brothers is, Can we all call each other Brother now?

Us brothers, both of us at the same time, both of us in one voice, we both tell Boy: No.

Now, it is clear to the both of us brothers, Boy wants more than just wanting Girl.

So what you're saying, we say to Boy, is that you want to be a brother to us brothers too?

Brother says, So you want us to call you Brother too?

At this, Boy wags his boy head, yes, yes.

If you can walk on water is what us brothers say to this.

And so what Boy does to us saying this is he turns and he walks out into the river.

Boy walks and he walks and he keeps on walking out until Boy is just a head floating on top of the water.

After a while, Boy is not even that.

After a while, Boy's head, Boy's whole body, it is swallowed up by the mouth that is the river's.

It's true that Boy drowned the first time he walked on water.

But then, Boy, Boy walked back upriver—back across the water, all the way back to us brothers.

And with him, that day, that was the day the river started flowing the other way.

We teach Boy how to fish, too—to bait his fishing hooks with a mixture of spit and mud.

On Boy's first cast, when he reels in his line, there are thirty thousand fish on the end of Boy's hook. There is a silvery bridge of fish stretching from one side of the river all the way across to the other side of the river, begging Boy to put them in his mud-rusty bucket.

When us brothers see this, we tell Boy that he is one foot closer to being one of us, but that he still has one foot in that other world, in the world that has nothing to do with us.

Tell me, Boy says. What else do I have to do?

Give us your hand, we say to Boy.

Boy does like he is told.

We are brothers.

We are what Boy wants to be.

We walk with Boy up from the river, back into the back of our backyard.

We back Boy back up against our backyard telephone pole, our back-of-the-yard fishing pole, us brothers like to call it—this pole that is creosote-coated and has hammered and nailed into its tarry black wood the chopped-off heads from all the fish that us brothers catch out of the dirty river that runs through this dirty river town.

Hold your hand, we tell Boy, up against this pole's wood.

Boy raises up his hand, not to say no, not to say stop, but to say yes, yes he can take it.

He can be a brother too is what Boy's hand is saying to us.

In my hands I am holding a hammer in one hand and a fist full of rusty, bent-back nails in the other.

This might sting, is what I say, and then I raise back the hammer. I drive that rusted nail right through Boy's hand.

Boy doesn't flinch, or wince with his boy body, or make with his boy mouth the sound of a boy crying out.

Good, Brother, the both of us brothers hear ourselves say.

When we hear each other say these words, the both of us brothers give each other that look. We look this look back and forth between each other, and then we turn this look to look it back at Boy.

Look now with us brothers as we look at this boy.

See Boy with us.

Boy is standing, back here in the back of our backyard, with his back and his boot heels backed up against this fish-headed telephone pole, and with his right hand raised up the way that it's raised up, and with this rusty nail running through it, Boy looks to us brothers like he could, yes he could, he could be one of us.

Now am I a brother now? is what Boy with his boy mouth says.

I don't say anything to this.

All I can do to this is this.

I raise back with the hammer again and I am hammering in a second nail into Boy's other hand when our father, it is our father, he steps out into the back of our backyard.

Boys, our father calls this word out.

Us brothers, we turn back our boy heads towards the sound of our father.

We wait for our father to say whatever it is that he is going to say to us brothers next.

It is a long few seconds.

The sky above the river where the steel mill sits shipwrecked in the river's edge mud, it is dark and quiet.

Somewhere, I am sure, the sun is shining.

You boys be sure to clean up before you come back in, is what our father tells us.

Our father turns back his back.

Us brothers turn back to face back our faces back at this boy.

Now can I have Girl? is what this boy says.

Us brothers, we are looking into this boy's face.

This boy's face, when we are looking into it like this, it is almost like we are looking at each other.

Boy is all that us brothers have for ourselves to say.

There is no other way for us to say it.

Boy.

And I raise back the hammer.

I line up that rusted nail.

Fish Heads: Revisited

We hit.

We kept on hitting.

We did not stop with this hitting for twenty-three days and nights.

We hit.

For twenty-three days, for twenty-three nights, we hit.

We could not stop with this hitting until this fish that we were hitting was hit over the top of the head dead.

We couldn't believe it, this fish, it was the longest we had ever before seen a fish out of the water keep on breathing.

This fish, it held on. It kept on breathing. It did not want to stop living in this out of the water world.

But us brothers, we wanted this fish's fishy head.

It would look good, us brothers knew, this fish's fish head—we could picture it—up at the tip-top of our fish-headed telephone pole out back in the back of our backyard.

This fish's head, it was the biggest fish head either one of us brothers had ever before with our boy eyes seen.

Our eyes did not lie.

Our eyes told us what our hands were already knowing.

Our backyard telephone pole, the pole with all of those fish heads hammered and nailed into that wood pole's creosoted blackness, that pole needed this fish head to be up at its peak.

And so we hit.

We hit with our fists.

We hit at this fish with our hands balled into fists, our fists wrenched around hammers.

We took turns hitting.

We took turns hitting this fish.

Like this.

And this.

This fish, it took whatever us brothers had to give it.

It did not, this fish, want to be just a head.

It did not want to be, this fish, because of us brothers, just one of a hundred-and-fifty fish heads that us brothers hammered and nailed into our fish-headed telephone pole out back in the back of our backyard.

But after twenty-three days and twenty-three nights of us brothers doing this hitting, this fish, it took its last breath.

It died.

It died the way that we know that nothing ever really does.

It kept on living.

We fished out a knife from our front trouser pockets. We chopped off this fish's head.

This fish's fishy eyes, they never stopped staring.

Look how the eyes on this fish keep on staring.

Not even the stars could out shine such shining.

Like stars, we gave each of these fishes' eyes each a name.

Not one was called Jimmy or John.

Jimmy and John was mine and my brother's name.

We called each other Brother.

Brother, I said to Brother. You can go first.

I gave Brother this look.

There was a look that, us brothers, we sometimes liked to look at each other with this look. It was the kind of a look that hurt the eyes of the brother who was the one of us doing the looking.

Imagine that look.

Open up your eyes up good and wide, I said to Brother.

What are you saying? Brother said.

Hold your head, I said to Brother, up close to this pole's fish-headed wood.

Brother did just like I told.

Look: we were brothers.

We were each other's voice inside our own heads.

This might sting, I warned, and I reached back with the hammer, I drove that rusted nail right through Brother's eye.

Brother didn't blink, or wince with his body, or make with his boy mouth the sound of a brother crying out.

Good, Brother, I said.

I was hammering in the second nail into Brother's other eye when our father stepped out into the back of our backyard.

Sons, our father called this word out.

Us brothers, us, our father's sons, we turned back our boy heads towards the sound of our father.

We waited to hear what it was that our father was going to say to us brothers next.

It was a long few seconds.

The sky above the river down where the steel mill was a shipwrecked ship, it was dark and quiet.

Somewhere, I was sure, the sun was shining.

You boys remember to clean up before you come back in, our father said.

Our father turned back his back.

Us brothers turned to face back with each other.

Look, I said.

I raised back the hammer.

Look again.

I lined up that rusted nail.